T0365894

The Adventures of Sydney Snow Jr

Written by:
Rosemary Szeiler

Illustrated by: **Dwight Nacaytuna**

JOY
Population : 649

ISBN: Softcover   978-1-5144-6037-5
        Hardcover   978-1-5144-6038-2
        EBook   978-1-5144-6036-8

Print information available on the last page

Rev. date: 02/12/2016

To order additional copies of this book, contact:
Xlibris
1-888-795-4274
www.Xlibris.com
Orders@Xlibris.com

The Adventures of Sydney Snow Jr

Written by:
Rosemary Szeiler
Illustrated by: Dwight Nacaytuna

In a magical snow-covered land where the snow is always plentiful and beautiful; there lived Sydney Snow Jr. who was the son of Sydney Snow Sr. and Cindy Snow; the most loving parents to ever live in the town of Burr in the Northlands.

Sydney was a happy snow lad, and he worked hard and he was very respectful. His parents are very proud of their son. The snow people of this land were enchanted by a kind wizard named Cecil, and he was married to Josephine a good witch.

The Snow family would enjoy time together going on outings and picnics. Cindy Snow would pack a picnic basket of homemade frozen fried chicken and frozen yogurt. On one particular day Jack Frost who also lived in Burr, and as we all know he has a temper. Mr. Frost had an argument with Mrs. Frost because she spent a little too much on a big sale at the department store.

He, as often he does lost his temper. Well he caused a very big and unexpected storm, but it was over quickly because he cannot stay angry with his dear wife for long. As it happens, the Snow family was on a picnic that very day when that sudden storm hit. The three of them were trying to get to safety in a nearby cave. Sydney Jr. was in back of his parents trying to get them there as quick as he could. He could hardly see through the snow, but he saw the cave opening enough to give them both a push forward. They were both safely inside the cave, but Sydney Jr. stumbled, and a rogue wind picked him up and swirled him into it. He traveled in this wind for a long while until it finally dropped him in an unfamiliar place.

A pretty town with quaint stores and decorated trees; he was on a hill overlooking the houses and stores. He could see the townsfolk busy and hurrying about, for the holidays are a busy time of year.

Sydney knew he was lost and needed help. He ventured closer to the town, and on his way he read a sign that said JOY population 649. Now he knew he was a stranger in a strange land, and he became a little afraid. He remembered his parents teaching him to be brave and always have faith. These thoughts cheered him up, and he set out to find help.

He was hiding by a building quietly observing the activities of the town inhabitants. A little girl with long blonde hair and the bluest of eyes was wearing a heavy coat with boots, gloves, scarf and hat. She was prepared for an ice age. She walked up behind him and startled him, and she was surprised when he moved because Alyssa knew snowmen didn't move!

Meanwhile back in Burr Sydney Sr. and Cindy were beside themselves with worry. Where was their son, and was he alright, and will they ever see him again? They went straight to Sheriff Brisk who immediately set up a search party to find Sydney Jr. He organized all the deputies and volunteers including the snow dogs. Poor Cindy was crying and her tears turned into little frozen teardrops. Mr. and Mrs. Snow tried to comfort each other, but they both feared the worst.

Elsa their neighbor and Cindy's best friend who happened to be a gingerbread lady suggested they speak to Cecil the wizard, for maybe he could help. They donned their hats and gloves, and Cindy grabbed her purse and off they went to see Cecil and his wife Josephine. They found them at home and explained the situation. Josephine went to consult her crystal ball, and she saw Sydney Jr, and she could see he was very much alive and well. But where was he, and how will they get him home?

In Joy the two of them just looked at each other, and then Sydney spoke. "Hello miss my name is Sydney Snow Jr.".

Alyssa was not sure how to address a talking snowman, but she called him sir as she was a polite girl.

Alyssa said, "Hello sir my name is Alyssa, and I've never met a talking snowman before."

"It is nice to meet you Alyssa. Where I come from in Burr all snow people and gingerbreads talk," he said.

She asked if he went to school, and he said of course doesn't everyone? This was the beginning of a special friendship.

They both had so many things to ask of each other and learn about each other's cultures. He shared his story of how he was lost and needed help to get home. She thought about how she could help him with his dilemma. She decided the first thing she had to do was find her brother Alec. He was smart and always knew what to do.

Alyssa said to Sydney, "Please wait here, and I will get my brother Alec ". She returned in a few minutes with a very confused brother, for he could not understand what his sister was telling him.

Alyssa introduced her brother to Sydney Jr. and they had fun getting to know each other. They decided to show their knew friend the town and the park.

As they went through town everyone looked with surprise at a snowman with life and movement and speech. Sydney greeted everyone, and all who met him were impressed and happy to spend time with him. The town welcomed him into their community, and the children loved playing with him especially in the park. He would pull them on their sleigh. What fun for everyone!

Jose was watching from his room at the children playing and having fun. He knew about the lively snowman, for news travels quickly in the town of Joy. He was not able to walk, and his wheelchair couldn't get him through the snow to be with all of his friends in the park.

Isabella who is a spirited and bright girl with dark hair and I can do anything attitude realized with guilt that her brother was alone in his room, and she stopped playing. She thought about how she could introduce her brother Jose to Sydney, but she couldn't think of anything.

Then she realized that perhaps she could bundle him up with her mother's help, and get him in the sleigh so Sydney could pull him. Then he could be part of the festivities, and she made it happen. Now, all of the children were playing and having fun. Sydney Snow was having the time of his life with his new friends, and he almost forgot his problems.

When evening fell and the children and all of the townsfolk were in there homes with their families. Sydney stayed outside looking up at the stars eating a frozen spaghetti dinner he was given by his new friends. He had to refuse the offers of dinner from most of the town, for snowmen need to be outdoors in the cold.

He looked at the stars and thought about his parents, and he hoped they weren't worrying about him. He also thought about Juliette the most beautiful snow maiden in the world in his eyes. Her eyes were blue which is rare for snow people, but she was part Italian Ice on her mother's side.

As the days came and went there was fun for all, and Sydney Snow became a bit of a celebrity. He even had the local news interview him, and they filmed him putting the star on top of the town Christmas tree.

It was always fun during the day because there was so much to do. At night Sydney felt the loneliness for his family and friends back home in Burr. He especially missed Juliette, for he wants to ask her to marry him.

In the mornings the local coffee shop was overflowing with the citizens of Joy enjoying their morning coffee with Sydney Jr. He especially liked iced coffee and the children would drink orange juice. Then it was off to the park for more fun and games. Sydney brought so much joy to the town of Joy with a population of 649 + 1.

It was getting closer to Christmas with each passing day, and the children asked if Sydney had a Christmas wish. He heard all of their wants and wishes, and he hoped that all of theirs was granted, but his only wish was to be with his family and friends in Burr, and to see his Juliette with her smile.

Although the children all loved their new snow friend, they also realized it would be selfish to keep him in Joy, for they wanted their friend to be happy.

Now they had to figure out a way to get Sydney home in time for Christmas. After all Christmas is a time for thinking of others and their happiness.

Isabella gathered the children together to solve the problem of getting Sydney home in time for Christmas. Alyssa suggested they shoot him out of a cannon facing north, but Isabella told her that may not be a safe idea. The boys Alec and Michael thought a helicopter could get him there in time.

Jose suggested they speak to Mr. Scott the life flight helicopter pilot, and so the children set out to find Mr. Scott Jones. They found him working on his helicopter. He greeted them warmly, for he always enjoyed visits with the local children. He believes that children are our future so he felt time with them was important.

He listened intently to the challenge of getting Sydney home, but he explained that a helicopter has to refuel every two to three hours, and there was no place to refuel his helicopter between Joy and Burr. Also he wasn't exactly sure where Burr was.

Back north in the township of Burr all of the town was still upset that Sydney Jr was somewhere, and Josephine the good witch was studying her crystal ball, and she was able to discover that Sydney was south in a place called Joy very far away. She told Cecil her husband what she knew, and they went to the library to study maps stored there. After many hours of research they knew his location, but how will they get him home. They took all of their information to the town elders to devise a plan.

At the same time in Joy the children all went to city hall and requested an audience with the mayor. Her name was Amelia, and she was a very resourceful and compassionate woman who always put the residents of her town first. She was also a very pretty and proud woman who was very stylish and trendy. The children felt sure she would have answers to help Sydney.

As the dilemma was presented to her she took notes, and after she thought about the problem for a while she picked up the phone, and she called for a town meeting for all craftsmen and seamstresses and engineers.

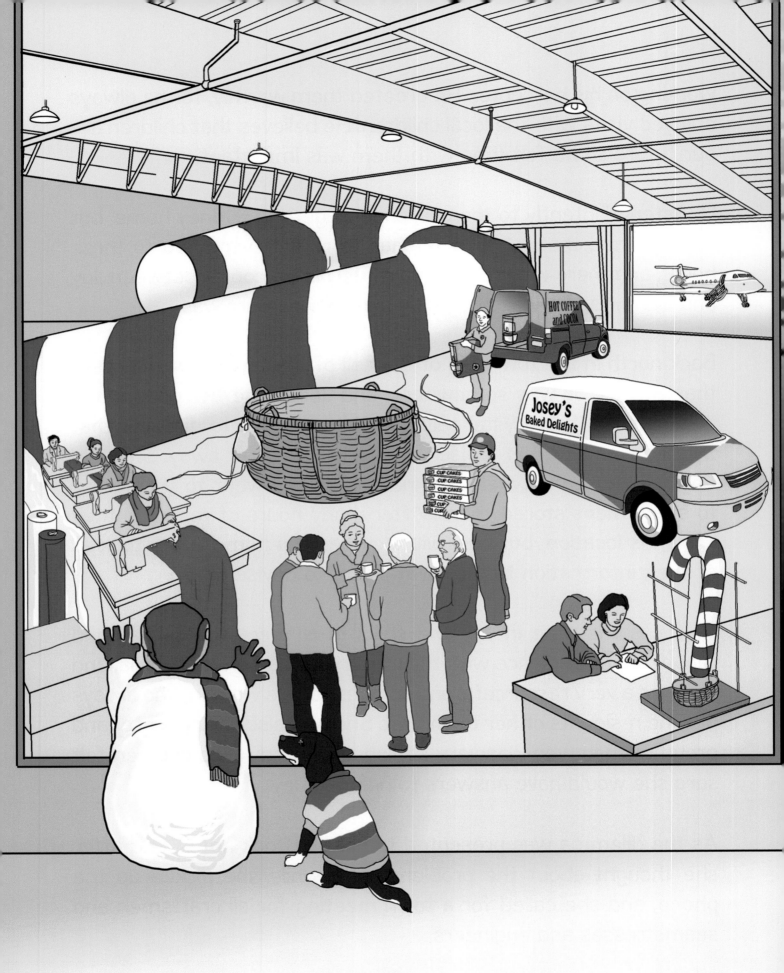

At the meeting Miss. Amelia told everyone that she wanted a balloon constructed for Sydney Jr, and this hot air balloon would carry him home safely. The men and women in attendance were eager to help, and they pooled their resources to make this hot air balloon project happen. The engineers made sure that the hot air dispenser was safely above Sydney.

Now the first problem was getting the material needed for the huge balloon and what color? They tried to order it, but it would take too long to deliver it. Scott the helicopter pilot offered to fly down to pick it up as that would save time, and he was always ready to set out on a mission. So he grabbed his gear, and headed out to his helicopter to bring back the material needed. The color chosen was red and white stripes like a candy cane, for everyone loves a candy cane.

The weather was clear for his flight to bring back the material. He had to stop and refuel a couple of times, but he returned with the fabric as quick as he could.

The craftsmen were prepared with all of the equipment and tools needed for the balloon project.

The ladies of the quilting club were seated at their sewing machines which were set up in a hanger at the airport. It was getting very close to Christmas, and all of the sewing machines were running, and everyone was involved with the project. The local coffee shop delivered coffee and hot cocoa, and the sandwich shop brought over fresh deli creations and for desert cupcakes for everyone from Josey's baked delights. The whole town was working together, and there was a team spirit that made everyone happy, for it always feels good to do something for someone.

Sydney would watch the progress of his transportation home through the windows. One day a young stray dog came up to him. She was hungry and cold but very friendly. He found her some food, and Michael's mother was able to make her a knitted sweater out of left over yarn, and so she had a multicolored sweater to keep warm. She followed Sydney everywhere, and she played with all of the children. She brought so much happiness to them, and they had to give her a name.

Sydney Jr said, "She brings us so much happiness we should call her Happy." Everyone agreed, and she was the happiest little black dog with white markings on her feet in all of Joy.

Now no one was thinking about saying goodbye, for everyone was busy and having fun.

The wizard Cecil wrote a note to send to Sydney, for he knew how to bring the young snowman home. He attached the note to Irisa, a gentle dove, and he gave her directions to get to Sydney.

Then Cecil and his wife Josephine went to visit Jack Frost. After all this whole mess, was his fault, and he needed to help fix it.

They knocked on Jack's door and Mrs. Frost answered. She was a warm and delightful lady with lots of patience to put up with Jack. When Cecil the wizard found Jack in his study he said, "Jack we have a problem, and you need to help."

Jack was very sorry for the trouble he caused and promised to help in any way. Jack felt sure he could make a wind to bring Sydney home, for Josephine knew what they were doing to construct a hot air balloon, for she was watching in her crystal ball. She liked being a good witch, for she loved having magical talents.

Irisa, the dove, was flying as fast as she could through some wintery weather, and she was getting tired, but she was determined to get Sydney her friend the message.

Irisa was flying over Joy and spotted Sydney below playing with his new friends and a little dog. She landed near him, and he recognized her right away. He gave her a big hug, and introduced her to everyone. She said, "It is very nice to meet all of you." The children were surprised to meet a dove with such good manners and speech. She was also enchanted by the wizard, for he enchanted all who were in Burr. The note said - Sydney we miss you, and we are fine. Jack can get you home as soon as the balloon is in the air.-

The balloon was almost finished, and it was planned to be ready to fly Christmas morning so he was able to enjoy the Christmas Eve party. The biggest party of the year, and he was trying to decide which scarf to wear.

Finally, the balloon was finished, and it was set out and tied down ready for take off. It was now Christmas Eve, and it was time for the big party. Everyone was there, and there was music, dancing, mistletoe, and food. Happy the little dog was so excited to be part of all the fun. She finally found someone to belong to, for all dogs want to belong to someone, and her someone was Sydney Snow Jr.

In the morning the whole town showed up to see the balloon take Sydney and Irisa, the dove high up into the sky. There were so many tears saying goodbye, and Sydney was presented a key to the city, for he promised to visit every year in the winter, and he hoped to bring his Juliette to meet them next year.

Happy did not know what was going on, but she didn't like her Sydney in a hot air balloon. She was barking and jumping to get to him, but Sydney was leaving without her because Burr was cold year round, and she was better off in Joy.

Happy was realizing that Sydney was leaving her, and her heart was breaking. The children handed Happy up to Sydney for one last hug, and the ropes broke free. The balloon was airborne, and Happy was with Sydney and Irisa, and Happy new that no matter what adventures lie ahead she had a home.

Jack Frost sent a very strong wind as soon as the balloon was high enough, and everyone on the ground was holding on to their hats.

In a couple of hours the balloon landed in Burr, and all of his family and friends were there to greet him. So many hugs, kisses, and so much to talk about.

When his eyes met Juliette he knew she is the one he wants to marry, but that is another story.

Happy the stray little dogs wish came true, and she had a home, and Sydney loved having Happy with him and he would make sure she had a wardrobe of sweaters.

Sydney shared concerns with the wizard Cecil that he would miss his friends, but Cecil promised that Jack Frost would wind power his balloon anytime he wanted to visit his friends in Joy.

Sydney Snow Jr enriched the lives of the people in Joy, and he was a loved member of his hometown. He was glad he got to meet his new friends, and he was glad to be home. Now he felt he had two homes, and he had much to celebrate and be thankful for.

What a wonderful holiday season. Merry Christmas and Happy Holidays to everyone!

P.s. Jack Frost was court ordered to go to anger management classes!

THE END
To David (aka Sydney Jr)